MITZI's
Honeymoon With
Nana Potts

MITZI's Honeymoon With Nana Potts

by Barbara Williams

illustrated by Emily Arnold McCully

E. P. Dutton   New York

Library of Congress Cataloging in Publication Data

Williams, Barbara.
Mitzi's honeymoon with Nana Potts.

Summary: Eight-year-old Mitzi has always wanted
a grandmother, but her new stepbrothers' grandmother,
who wears wigs and insists on healthy foods, is not
exactly what Mitzi had in mind.
    [1. Grandmothers—Fiction. 2. Stepchildren—Fiction.
3. Family life—Fiction] I. McCully, Emily Arnold, ill.
II. Title.
PZ7.W65587Mj 1983 [Fic] 83-14086
ISBN 0-525-44078-X

Published in the United States by E. P. Dutton, Inc.,
2 Park Avenue, New York, N.Y. 10016

Published simultaneously in Canada by
Fitzhenry & Whiteside Limited, Toronto

Editor: Ann Durell   Designer: Claire Counihan

Printed in the U.S.A.   COBE   First Edition

10 9 8 7 6 5 4 3 2 1

for
Joe, who had to spend his parents' honeymoon
with Grandma Williams
and for our two newest grandchildren,
Christopher Wright Williams
and
Jody Sanders

Contents

1

The Dinosaur Alarm Clock

BAM! A painful weight landed on Mitzi's stomach. What awful thing had happened in the dark? An earthquake? A plane crash?

No. She opened one sleepy eye and saw three-year-old Darwin straddling her middle.

"Grunch," said Darwin, making his favorite tyrannosaurus rex noise and bouncing again on Mitzi's stomach.

"Ugh," groaned Mitzi. "I can't breathe."

"Grunch, grunch, grunch," replied the dinosaur cheerfully, springing up and down.

Wearily Mitzi pushed him to one side on her bed. Only yesterday, just before the wedding, Mitzi's mother had hugged her and said, "It's going to be fun for all of us to belong to a wonderful big family."

But trying to get used to a house full of strangers was not fun. Being left home when her mother and stepfather went on a two-week honeymoon to the beach was not fun. Being awakened before daylight by a bounce on the stomach was not fun.

By himself, Mitzi's new father might have been all right. Walter Potts was a biology professor who also liked to hammer and saw. He had just built a big bedroom and bath on Mitzi's house. More important, he was the one who decided that Mitzi could go on an archaeology field trip with her mother, just as soon as the honeymooners returned.

But new fathers were supposed to join your family by themselves. They weren't supposed to bring a whole family with them—two sons and the boys' grandmother.

Mitzi knew all about grandmothers. She didn't remember her own very well, but she had learned about them from her friends, especially her best friend, Elsie Wolf. Grandmothers were people who invited you to dinner on Easter and Thanksgiving. They took you to the ballet on your birthday and knitted you sweaters for Christmas. They smelled like rose gardens and peppermint candy when they kissed you. And Mitzi really wanted one.

She thought it was unfair for Elsie Wolf to have two grandmothers when she, Mitzi, had none.

Nana Potts didn't count. She wasn't a real grandmother. Nana Potts was just a silly lady who happened to be the mother of Mitzi's new stepfather—the lady who got the big bedroom Walter had built on Mitzi's house. (Why didn't Mitzi get that bedroom? Or her mother? It was their house, wasn't it?) Nana Potts was someone who thought Darwin was adorable even when he was being awful. Nana Potts was someone who thought everyone's name but her own was *we*.

Take last night, after the wedding, for instance. Before Walter and her mother drove off on their honeymoon, they gave all the children presents. Mitzi's was a shiny green bathrobe that she was so eager to wear she got undressed early. But Darwin cried to wear it so he would look like a tyrannosaurus rex. "Why don't we be a nice big sister and let Darwin borrow our bathrobe?" Nana Potts suggested. But she didn't mean her own bathrobe. She meant Mitzi's.

Then eleven-year-old Frederick went into the living room to watch a "Dallas" rerun. "Why don't we play Monopoly with our little sister?" Nana Potts urged. But Nana Potts didn't want to play Monopoly with Mitzi. She wanted to watch "Dallas" herself.

Now it was morning (or *almost* morning), and Darwin the dinosaur was jouncing Mitzi's bed so hard she couldn't sleep. Her room, her house— all the things Mitzi had once shared only with her mother—had been taken over by strangers. Crazy strangers.

3

Darwin smacked the mattress beside Mitzi's head. "Get up!" he ordered. "It's time for our honeymoon!"

"Only married people get honeymoons," complained Mitzi. She remembered how unjust that had seemed when her mother tried to explain it.

"Uh-uh," argued Darwin. "We're going to have a honeymoon while Daddy and Mommy are away."

Mitzi frowned. Somehow it didn't seem right for Darwin to call her mother Mommy. He should call her Patricia, the way Frederick did. Better still, he should call her mother Pat.

"While Daddy and Mommy are away," Darwin repeated, "you and Frederick and Nana and I are going to have a honeymoon together. Nana said so."

"Well, it's too early for a honeymoon now," said Mitzi. She was eight and knew more than a preschooler like Darwin. "Go back to bed."

"I want breakfast!" cried Darwin. He scrambled next to her so their noses nearly touched and held his fists like claws. "I'm a tyrannosaurus rex. Feed me or I'll eat *you*!"

BANG! BANG! BANG! came a noise from downstairs. Mitzi sat up, startled. "What's that?"

"Just Frederick hammering," said Darwin.

"Hammering?" wailed Mitzi. "It's too early to hammer."

4

"Daddy says you should build early so you will build with joy," said Darwin.

"Huh?" said Mitzi. "What does that mean?" She thought it sounded dumb. Mitzi lay down and closed her eyes.

"Don't you know either?" asked Darwin.

"No," said Mitzi, who was now sure it was dumb. She also thought it was dumb that people believed a three-year-old like Darwin was a genius just because he repeated every stupid thing he ever heard. "Go tell Frederick to fix you something to eat," suggested Mitzi.

"He won't. He's hammering," said Darwin.

"Well, I'm sleeping," said Mitzi.

"No, you're not," argued Darwin. "You're talking."

"Well, I *want* to sleep," said Mitzi. "Go tell Nana Potts to fix you something."

"She's gone," said Darwin.

Mitzi sat up again, frightened. What terrible thing had caused Nana Potts to leave, before it was even morning? "Gone?" asked Mitzi. "Where?"

"Back to our old house to help the movers. They're bringing the rest of our stuff today."

"Oh," said Mitzi, lying down again. She felt relieved but at the same time annoyed. If Nana Potts thought that she and Frederick and Darwin and Mitzi were having a honeymoon together,

5

why didn't Nana Potts stay home and *have* it?

"GRUNCH!" howled Darwin, bouncing the bed again. "Nana said you would be a nice sister and fix my breakfast."

Hmmph, thought Mitzi, who suddenly felt her stomach roll. She wished Nana Potts hadn't suggested she fix breakfast because a dish of Choco Crispies would have tasted very good right then. But she didn't want to fix breakfast because Nana Potts suggested it. Only if she thought of it herself.

Suddenly Mitzi felt a small hand patting her cheek. "Nice sister," said Darwin. "Please fix my breakfast."

It was more than Mitzi could resist.

"Oh, all right," she said. "But only if you promise to let me sleep in every day for the rest of the honeymoon."

"I promise," Darwin bubbled.

Mitzi got out of bed and staggered to the closet for her slippers.

"What's sleeping in?" asked Darwin.

"Sleeping late. Until after the sun is up," explained Mitzi. She was planning how she'd ask Walter to put a lock on her door just as soon as he came home from the honeymoon. If Darwin wouldn't bother her until then, she'd be safe forever more. "You promised you'd let me do that every day for the next two weeks."

"I will," said Darwin brightly. "Just like I did today." He pointed to the window. "See, the sun is up now."

Mitzi started to yell at him. Then she remembered something her mother had told her yesterday. "I hope you'll be a big girl and help Nana Potts while Walter and I are gone." It pleased Mitzi to think of acting like a big girl and helping.

Nana Potts always called Darwin adorable when he tried to help, even though he never did it very well. But Mitzi was big enough to be really useful. Wouldn't Nana Potts be pleased when she realized that?

Mitzi leaned over to get her slippers.

"Hey!" she yelled. Darwin had slipped a rope around her neck.

"Giddyup, Brontosaurus!" commanded Darwin, shaking the ends.

"Stop that!" choked Mitzi. "I can't breathe."

Darwin loosened the reins slightly but continued to shake them. "Downstairs, Brontosaurus. Fast. The mean Tyrannosaurus Rex wants breakfast."

2

The Orange Juice Disaster

When she reached the kitchen, Mitzi dropped the rope Darwin had put around her neck on the floor by the counter. Darwin had already wandered off to the living room to watch Frederick hammer.

On the kitchen table was a sealed envelope addressed to Mitzi. She opened it eagerly and grew even more excited when a twenty dollar bill fell out. How wonderful of her mother to leave Mitzi this extra surprise before she went on her honeymoon! Then Mitzi unfolded the paper and read the note, printed in large letters:

Dear Mitzi,
Would we like to cook for our brothers
this morning? Patricia didn't leave
much food, so here is some money to go
to the store. (We won't buy any junk
food or toys, will we?) I've gone to
the old house to help the movers.

Love,
Nana Potts

Mitzi was no longer pleased. Why didn't Nana Potts come right out and say what she meant instead of always hinting around. Why did she keep calling Mitzi *we*? Where did she get the nerve to say that Mitzi's mother didn't leave much food? Her mother had left wonderful food—delicious sandwiches and pastries from the wedding reception. Of course, Mitzi and Frederick had eaten all of them last night.

"Yow!" cried Mitzi, spinning around. Frederick had come into the room when she wasn't looking and had read the note over her shoulder. "You scared me!"

"Sorry," he replied with a shrug. He was wearing a green T-shirt that said SAVE THE WHALES. All Frederick's T-shirts had messages on them.

Frederick appeared to be studying a spot on the ceiling, but Mitzi knew he wasn't really looking at anything. He was just getting ready to give her a speech.

"Nana is very big on written directives," Frederick began.

Mitzi didn't interrupt, even though she wanted to. What were *written directives*? she wondered.

"She leaves notes all over the house," he explained. " 'Frederick, Don't waste our glass of milk.' 'Darwin, This toothbrush wants us to use it.' "

Frederick smiled at Mitzi. He always looked at

her like that when it was time for her to laugh. Mitzi smiled too, even though she didn't see anything funny.

Frederick removed the thick, horn-rimmed glasses from his nose. He huffed noisily on one lens before rubbing it with a tissue from his pocket. "I suppose I should have agreed to fix breakfast. But I thought Nana would stay home and do it herself if I reminded her about my accordion lesson. I wanted to finish hanging a hook before my lesson. But I'll fix breakfast if you don't know how."

Of course she knew how to fix breakfast. "I can do it," Mitzi said.

Frederick shrugged. "Okay," he said, putting his glasses back on his nose. "Call me if you need help," he added over his shoulder as he walked out the door.

Hmmph, thought Mitzi. She would show Frederick she could fix breakfast. And Nana Potts, too. She would show everyone what a good helper she was. She would fix Frederick and Darwin the best breakfast they had ever eaten. And she would do it without going to the store to buy more food. So there!

She yanked open the kitchen linen drawer and reached under the old plastic placemats for three yellow cloth ones. Mitzi set them on the kitchen table, smiling because it would serve Nana Potts right when Darwin spilled on the mats and she had to wash them. Bolder now, Mitzi made another decision. She opened the drawer again and got out three cloth napkins. There! Nana Potts could wash those, too! Mitzi hummed softly as she got out the silverware and finished setting the table.

Now for the food. In the bread box were only two pieces of bread, both spotted with green mold. That meant she couldn't fix toast. In the refrigerator, Mitzi found only a few spoonfuls of milk in the big plastic bottle. That meant she couldn't fix cold cereal. Toast and cold cereal were Mitzi's favorite breakfast and the only things she knew how to cook. She bit her lip, thinking hard.

Some distance away, in the living room, Frederick and Darwin were quarreling.

"Come on, Darwin," said Frederick. "What did you do with it?"

"You always say I take everything," said Darwin.

Mitzi didn't have time for other people's quarrels. She had problems of her own to worry about. Food. That's what she was worrying about. Let's see. She could serve soda crackers and peanut butter instead of toast. But she would still need something runny to pour on the cereal. What did they have that was runny? She bit her lip again.

11

Louder shouts came from the living room.

"I spent all morning putting up that hook," complained Frederick. "And now the macrame is gone. Where did you put it?"

"I didn't put it anywhere. I don't have it," said Darwin.

"Macrame doesn't just get up and walk away," argued Frederick.

Mitzi opened the door to the freezing compartment, hoping for an idea. Frozen orange juice! Why not? She had never tasted it on Choco Crispies, but that didn't mean it wouldn't be good. And orange juice was almost her specialty. She had watched her mother make it lots of times. All you did was open the can and pour the juice into a pitcher with some water.

As she peeled off the twirly white thing that released the lid, Mitzi hummed again. Fixing breakfast for your brothers made you feel grown up and important.

The frozen orange juice thumped into the pitcher. Mitzi turned on the faucet and filled the pitcher with water. She stirred the juice and then frowned. Somehow it didn't look as dark as the juice her mother made. She took a sip and frowned again. It didn't taste like the juice her mother made either. Anxiously she stirred some more. She had to think of some way to fix it.

Food coloring! Maybe that was it. Mitzi carried

a chair to the counter and climbed on it. She opened the cupboard door and pushed spices and herb teas this way and that, searching frantically. When she grabbed the box of food coloring, a large tin of peppercorns sailed past her ear and clattered to the floor, spraying the linoleum with black balls.

"Ooh!" Mitzi howled.

As footsteps thundered toward her, Mitzi jumped to the floor and snatched the pepper tin. She hid it and the food coloring behind the pitcher before the kitchen door blew open.

"What happened?" asked Frederick.

"Nothing," said Mitzi, who wished people would remember she was big enough to fix breakfast without any help.

"See," said Darwin, pointing. "I told you Mitzi took your macrame." The rope he had put around Mitzi's neck lay on the floor amid a swirl of peppercorns, like a snake mowed down by little black BB shot.

Frederick picked up the macrame between stiff fingers and eyed the floor with distaste. "What are those things?"

"Maybe it's bunny do-do," Darwin suggested brightly.

Frederick frowned. "There aren't any rabbits in here," he said. Even so, he held the macrame at a distance.

"It's just pepper," said Mitzi. She brushed the rope with her hand to show there was nothing to be afraid of. "It won't hurt anything," she told Frederick. "And I didn't know that was your rope. Darwin gave it to me."

"I did not give it to you," said Darwin. "It's Daddy's and Mommy's plant holder that Frederick made them for a wedding present. You can't have it."

Hmmph, thought Mitzi. She didn't want the old rope. Did Frederick really think she had taken it? Everything was going wrong, and it was all Nana Potts' fault. If Nana Potts had stayed home and watched Darwin—if Nana Potts had stayed home and fixed breakfast—none of Mitzi's problems would have happened.

"I knew you wouldn't take it," Frederick told Mitzi.

That made Mitzi feel a little better. "Well, you two go hang the plant holder, and I'll fix breakfast."

"Are you sure you don't need any help?" asked Frederick.

"No thank you," said Mitzi, eager to have the boys leave.

"She does too need help," said Darwin. He scowled at his left index finger, the one he always sucked. He had just stuck it in the pitcher to taste what Mitzi was making. "This orange juice tastes funny. It looks funny, too."

15

"Of course it tastes funny after you stick your slobbery finger in it. Come on and leave Mitzi alone." Frederick grabbed Darwin by the hand and yanked him out of the room.

Mitzi held her breath while their footsteps retreated. Now that Frederick's problem was solved, she must undertake a more difficult task— fixing the orange juice. You didn't have to be a three-year-old genius to know that it needed a lot of fixing.

Confident the boys were far away, Mitzi opened the box that held the little bottles of food coloring. Where's the orange, thought Mitzi, studying the four bottles—red, blue, green, and yellow. Well, red and yellow would make orange. Fortunately, Mitzi had mixed paints at school and knew all about colors. She removed the lids from the bottles, smearing red and yellow dye on her fingers.

In the living room, Frederick and Darwin were shouting again, louder than ever.

"You hurt Mitzi's feelings," accused Frederick. "Why can't you ever be polite?"

"Why can't you and Mitzi be polite?" demanded Darwin.

"Mitzi *is* being polite. She's making your breakfast. And you better eat every single bite of it and tell her it's delicious," Frederick threatened.

"I won't eat funny orange juice. Mitzi makes funny orange juice," said Darwin.

Mitzi's throat grew tight. She poured some of the red food coloring into the pitcher. *Clink, clink, clink,* stirred her spoon.

Why was the juice so dark? Would it lighten up when she poured in the yellow coloring? No. Together the red and yellow made a color like dirty rust. And the juice tasted as awful as ever.

Hastily Mitzi grabbed for the sugar bowl and dumped the contents into the pitcher. She stirred some more and then tasted the juice nervously. Phew! It was terrible. And her hands looked like two paint boxes. What could she do now?

"Mitzi's doing the best she can!" Frederick raged in the living room. "She can't help it if she isn't a genius like you."

Mitzi's stomach growled with hunger. But the rest of her body went stiff. Frederick was right. She wasn't a genius like him and Darwin. That must be why Nana Potts never said Mitzi was adorable. You couldn't be adorable if you were dumb.

Her hands shook as she took the pitcher and poured the contents down the sink. First the ugly rust liquid. Then a frozen lump of orange. Next she swept up the pepper and put it in the wastebasket. Finally she got the twenty dollar bill from the table.

Well. Being an adorable genius wasn't the only thing in the world. She would show Nana Potts. You didn't have to be a genius to be a good helper. She would show Frederick and Darwin that she could fix the best breakfast they ever ate.

And she would show Nana Potts that she had better ideas than any dumb genius.

3

Picnic Time

Mitzi was walking along University Street with her school tote bag full of food when she saw Frederick coming toward her. He was pulling his accordion case strapped to a wagon made from a sawed-off door on skateboards. *Rits, rits, rits,* came the wheels along the concrete.

Mitzi smiled. She could think of lots of uses for a neat wagon like that, beginning with pulling home the awkward bag of food she was carrying.

Frederick did not smile. "Boy, am I glad to see you," he said. But he sounded more tired than glad. "Darwin has been on a rampage since you left. Hunger pangs always put him on his worst D-minus behavior."

"Where *is* Darwin?" asked Mitzi. She couldn't see the Tyrannosaurus Rex anywhere.

"Home," said Frederick. Mitzi noticed he had changed to a clean red T-shirt. Black letters on it said BAN THE BOMB.

"Home?" repeated Mitzi, shocked. Frederick

shouldn't go off and leave a three-year-old. "Alone?" she asked.

"No, Nana and the movers are there. If Darwin hasn't eaten them by now." Frederick's nostrils twitched. In fact, he was sniffing. "Boy," he said, "what's in that tote bag?"

"Breakfast," said Mitzi proudly. "Come on back home and we can eat."

Frederick pointed to his cargo with an elbow. "Pulling this clumsy wagon Dad made for my accordion isn't exactly my idea of fun and games. Besides, if I take time to go back home, I'll be late for my music lesson. Don't you have something I can eat on my way?" He sniffed again. Noisily. "It smells terrific."

"It is terrific," said Mitzi, fishing a red and white striped box from the tote bag. "I bought us each a box of chicken from the Kentucky takeout. See?"

"Wow!" said Frederick. He let go of the wagon and took the box eagerly.

Mitzi grinned. Her breakfast was a success. "I bet you've never had Kentucky Fried Chicken for breakfast."

Frederick had already ripped into the box and taken a bite from a drumstick. "Nope," he agreed.

Giddy from her triumph, Mitzi felt talkative. "I bet no one has ever had Kentucky Fried Chicken for breakfast," she said. "I invented it myself. Just this morning." So there! Being a real helper was just as good as being an adorable genius.

Frederick nodded as he took another bite. "Great invention," he mumbled thickly. "Maybe the best I've ever tasted."

Well. Was it possible that Mitzi might be a genius after all? She wanted to hear Frederick say it. She wished he didn't have to go to his accordion lesson. "Why don't we sit down and eat here together?" she suggested. "We can put your accordion on the grass and use the wagon for a picnic table." Ah! Picnic table. She had invented something else.

Frederick checked his watch. "Okay," he said. He set down the box of chicken and began unstrapping the accordion case.

There wasn't room to put their legs under the wagon, so they sat cross-legged next to it, on the grass. Like Frederick, Mitzi chose to eat her drumstick first. She was chewing on it when she suddenly realized they weren't talking.

Talking with him had been the whole point. Besides, silence was unusual for Frederick. "What are you thinking?" Mitzi asked him.

"I've been counting how many times in my whole life I've eaten Kentucky Fried Chicken," Frederick said.

"How many?" Mitzi asked.

"Three," said Frederick.

"Whew," she sympathized softly. Mitzi, who ate from the takeout at least once a week, was an expert on Kentucky Fried Chicken. "There's gravy in that little cup," she told him. "Break your roll into pieces and dip it in the gravy."

Frederick ignored her suggestion and tilted back his head to stare at a cloud formation. "Once when I slept over at my friend's house. Once at a birthday party. And once when I had to baby-sit Darwin, and I took him to the zoo."

"You can buy mashed potatoes for the gravy, if you want them. But I got french fries today," said Mitzi. "That other cup has cole slaw. I hope you like cole slaw."

"Darwin said he was too tired to walk and cried for me to carry him," Frederick continued. "I sure didn't want to do that. I was trying to figure out if I had enough money for a taxi when, all of a sudden, I smelled this magnificent odor. I realized we were passing a Kentucky Fried Chicken restaurant and that if I took time right then to feed Darwin, he'd be able to walk. As my father always says, 'Use your brains and you won't have to use your brawn.' "

There Frederick went again. Talking about his own brains. Or Darwin's. He had not yet mentioned that Mitzi might be a genius for inventing Kentucky Fried Chicken for breakfast.

"Why have you had Kentucky Fried Chicken

only three times?" she asked, leading him back to the subject. "Doesn't Nana Potts like chicken?"

Frederick's drumstick was chewed almost dry. He selected another piece. For someone who didn't know much about the Colonel's takeout, Frederick could out-eat anyone Mitzi had ever met.

"Heck," Frederick said, "Nana specializes in chicken. She has two million recipes for cooking chicken. It's fast-food restaurants she doesn't like. Nana says, 'Time in your own kitchen may mean more pans to scrub, but it also means more vitamins to absorb.' "

Poor Frederick. Mitzi could imagine him spending his whole life in Nana Potts' kitchen, scrubbing pans and absorbing vitamins. Well, things would be better from now on.

"My mother loves fast-food restaurants," Mitzi assured him. "Now that our parents are married, you'll get Kentucky Fried Chicken all the time." Then a terrible thought hit her. Frederick and Darwin had probably never been on a picnic. How could you go on picnics if you didn't buy Kentucky Fried Chicken?

Mitzi decided to ask. "Doesn't Nana Potts ever take you on picnics?"

"Oh sure," said Frederick. "Nana's really hung up on picnics. We have them all the time."

Mitzi doubted that. Frederick just didn't want

her to feel sorry for him. "When?" she insisted.

Frederick shrugged, thinking. "Mostly in the summer, I guess. Now that school is out, Nana will fix lots of picnics for us."

Hmmph, thought Mitzi, who didn't like that idea at all. Picnics without Kentucky Fried Chicken! Imagine! But she was too polite to say what she was thinking. Instead, she decided to help Frederick figure it out for himself. "What's the best picnic you ever had?" she asked.

Frederick beamed. "That's easy."

Mitzi smiled, too. She knew he would say the picnic they were eating right then.

"Last summer on the Fourth of July," said Frederick.

"Oh," said Mitzi, deflated.

"We had fried chicken then, too," he told her.

Home-cooked, thought Mitzi. What kind of picnic was that? "Did you have french fries and gravy and cole slaw?" she challenged.

"No. We had fresh fruit salad and potato salad and chocolate eclairs and peanut butter popcorn balls."

"Oh," said Mitzi for the second time. She had never tasted peanut butter popcorn balls, and they sounded wonderful. Thinking about them, she realized that the takeout french fries she was eating were greasy. They were cold, too.

Besides fried chicken, Mitzi's favorite foods

25

were peanut butter and popcorn. And any lady who could put them together to make popcorn balls to eat at picnics might make a very nice grandmother. But of course Nana Potts would have to overcome all her faults first. Faults like calling Darwin adorable when he was just being clumsy or acting spoiled. Thinking Mitzi's name was *we*. Running off in the morning and expecting Mitzi to baby-sit. Yelling sometimes for no reason —like an old crab. Deciding fast-food restaurants were no good. Nana Potts was unfair.

Still, the french fries Mitzi had just bought really didn't taste very good. She pushed them aside, feeling disloyal.

"Hey, whose dog is that?" Frederick stood up nervously and looked at his watch.

A big Doberman pinscher was ambling toward them, sniffing the ground curiously.

"Oh, that's Rosie," said Mitzi. "She lives in the house on the corner of University Street. Here, Rosie!"

"Don't call her!" whispered Frederick. He jammed the lid shut on his chicken box. Then he picked up his accordion case to strap it back on the wagon.

"Why not?" asked Mitzi.

Frederick whispered again, as if he thought Rosie would eavesdrop. "There's a sign on that gate that says BEWARE OF DOG."

"Who cares?" said Mitzi, who was not fooled by signs. She knew Rosie's owners had posted that warning to keep people out of their fruit trees.

"RARF!" said Rosie.

"Now you've done it!" Frederick scolded. He worked anxiously at the accordion strap. "Just act calm, so she won't think you're scared."

How dare Frederick think she was afraid! "I'm not scared," Mitzi said.

"That's it," Frederick urged as he struggled with the buckle of his strap. "Just keep pretending you're calm, and the dog won't hurt you. Start walking toward home, and I'll watch to see that you're all right."

Mitzi was not pretending. She *was* calm. "YOU DON'T HAVE TO WATCH ME! I'M NOT SCARED!" she raged.

"Well, okay, if that's how you feel," said Frederick. "I've got to hurry, or I'll be late for my music lesson." He jerked at the wagon to make her think he was leaving. But he turned and looked at her over his shoulder.

"STOP WATCHING ME! I'M NOT A BABY!" Mitzi howled.

"Okay," said Frederick with another tug. "See you." He started off for real this time. *Rits, rits, rits.* He went farther. *Rits, rits, rrr . r . . r . . . r . . . .*

"Here, Rosie," called Mitzi. "Do you want me to scratch you?"

No. Rosie did not want to be scratched. She wanted Mitzi's tote bag. Seizing it in her teeth, Rosie dodged through some bushes and streaked toward her own house.

Mitzi dropped the box of fried chicken she had been eating to rescue the one still in the tote bag.

"Come back here!" yelled Mitzi, charging after Rosie. "That's Darwin's breakfast, you dumb dog! Give me back Darwin's breakfast!"

4

Flying High

Panting, Mitzi slammed into the front hall and dropped the tote bag she had rescued from Rosie on the floor. She was tired from hurrying and from carrying that bulky load so far.

"Darwin!" she huffed. "Where are you? Darwin?"

"Fly—ing, fly—ing," sang Darwin from the living room.

He sounded very cheerful—not at all like a tyrannosaurus rex on a rampage because of hunger pangs. Hmmph, thought Mitzi. Darwin had already eaten. She felt annoyed at Nana Potts for coming home first and giving Darwin breakfast. But Mitzi was even more annoyed at herself for stopping to talk to Frederick. It troubled her that she hadn't done a very good job of showing how helpful she could be by providing Darwin with something to eat when he was hungry.

Mitzi scowled at the tote bag and didn't even bother to pick it up as she walked into the living room.

"Darwin!" she cried when she saw him. Still in his pajamas, he had somehow climbed inside Frederick's macrame plant holder hanging from the ceiling and was sailing back and forth like a spider on a pendulum.

Seeing him, Mitzi felt old and wise. Didn't a genius, even a dumb one like Darwin, know better? The hook was not strong enough to hold anything as heavy as a boy. Especially when he was swinging back and forth that way.

"Does Nana Potts know what you're doing?" Mitzi asked.

Darwin didn't answer. Instead, he stuck his left index finger in his mouth and sucked furiously.

Mitzi realized at once that Nana Potts did not know what Darwin was doing.

"You're going to fall," Mitzi warned.

Darwin removed the finger from his mouth and grinned at her. "I'm not falling. I'm flying. Fly—ing, fly—ing, fly—"

Creak, creak, creak, went the hook Frederick had spent all morning hammering in place. Where was Nana Potts anyway? Frederick had said she was home. Why wasn't Nana Potts spending their honeymoon watching Darwin, the way she was supposed to?

"Get down," Mitzi commanded.

"I can't get down," Darwin answered cheerily. "The chair fell over."

A wooden chair underneath Darwin was lying on its side. Mitzi set it upright.

"There," she said. "Get down."

Darwin stretched out a chubby leg. On his next swing toward the chair, he pushed it over once more. "It fell over again," he squealed impishly and went back to sucking his finger.

Mitzi set the chair upright again. Darwin pushed it over again. Despite the finger in his mouth, Darwin giggled.

Mitzi, who usually enjoyed games, was not amused.

"I said get down!" she ordered, grabbing him.

"No!" shrieked Darwin.

"Ugh!" gasped Mitzi.

GR-R-RATE, went the hook as Mitzi and Darwin struggled. *GRATE, GRATE, GRATE.*

Mitzi let go. Force was not the answer. She had to think of something else. Yes. *Think.* Of course. Mitzi would prove to the world that she could out-think that dumb little genius if she just tried.

"Don't you want to know why I'm flying?" asked the dumb little genius.

Mitzi didn't answer. She had more important things to think about.

"Guess," demanded Darwin.

Mitzi said nothing.

Darwin apparently had stopped talking, too. Mitzi could hear him sucking his finger. He

31

sounded like a starving baby pig. Starving. That was it. Even if Nana Potts had fed Darwin, he was still hungry. Maybe Nana Potts hadn't fed him at all.

Mitzi rushed into the hall, snatched the canvas tote bag, and ran back into the living room where Darwin was flying. "If you'll get down, I'll give you your breakfast," she offered.

Darwin stopped swinging and sounded out the letters on the canvas bag. "A-me-li-a Ear-hart School. You don't have any breakfast in there," he accused. "That's just your school bag."

"Yes, I do," said Mitzi. She peeked inside and then smiled teasingly. "I have wonderful food in here. I bet you don't know what it is."

"It's just an old lunch sandwich left over from when you used to go to school," said Darwin. "I don't want an old leftover sandwich."

"No, it's not an old sandwich," said Mitzi. "It's a wonderful new kind of breakfast you've never tasted before. I invented it myself."

Darwin squinched up his face to consider that possibility. He seemed torn.

Mitzi removed the chicken box from the canvas bag with exaggerated gestures. "It's Kentucky Fried Chicken," she exclaimed. "I'm glad you don't want it."

"Give it to me," wailed Darwin. "I'm hungry! Nana said you have to give me breakfast."

Mitzi waved the box back and forth, out of Darwin's reach. "Not until you get down," she told him.

"Give it to me!" he howled. "I'm hungry."

Who cares, thought Mitzi wickedly. Darwin had behaved dreadfully all morning. It was only fair for him to suffer for a while.

"YOU BIG FAT ORANGE JUICE SPOILER!" Darwin raged. Angrily he tried to strike her.

Mitzi giggled. Now that she was winning, she decided that games with Darwin were fun.

Darwin's chin quivered, and his blue eyes filled with tears. Mitzi no longer felt like laughing. It was cruel for anyone as big and clever as she was to take advantage of a helpless little three-year-old.

She set the chicken box on the floor to free both her arms and reached toward Darwin, as a big sister should. "Here, I'll help you down."

That time, Darwin offered no resistance. When she set him on the floor, he grabbed the chicken box and ripped it open.

Well. Mitzi had provided her brothers with a breakfast they both loved. She was a good helper. Nana Potts could at least see that.

Now Mitzi would continue to show how responsible she was. She would sit with Darwin on the floor while he ate, to make certain he didn't get grease on the carpet.

Darwin snatched a drumstick in his small fist and bit off a hunk. "You didn't guess why I was flying," he mumbled thickly.

Mitzi felt generous. She would play his game.

"You were pretending to be a tyrannosaurus rex," she suggested.

"YOU OLD DUMMY!" he hooted, spraying the carpet with slobbery bits of meat.

Mitzi eyed the mess with distaste, then began picking at it with a paper napkin.

"TYRANNOSAURUS REXES CAN'T FLY!" Darwin bellowed.

Of course Mitzi knew that tyrannosaurus rexes couldn't fly. She was not an old dummy. "Well, you are a slimy stink beetle," said Mitzi, as she put the disgusting napkin in the takeout box.

Darwin did not seem to mind being a slimy stink beetle. "I'll give you a hint," he offered. "I can fly and I begin with a *P.*"

"A pterodactyl!" said Mitzi triumphantly. There. She had known that although the name of those flying dinosaurs began with a *T* sound, it was really spelled with a *P.* Darwin's stupid game was over, and she had won.

"No!" squealed Darwin. "Guess again."

Cheater! thought Mitzi, who was certain she had guessed correctly and that Darwin had changed the rules of his game as soon as he had lost. People did that sometimes. Cheaters like

Darwin. Well, she would not play his game any longer.

"Guess again," he urged.

"I don't want to," said Mitzi.

"You don't want to because you can't," challenged Darwin.

Where was Nana Potts anyway? It was her job to sit with Darwin while he ate.

"Guess," insisted Darwin.

"A parrot," blurted Mitzi.

"Wrong again," howled Darwin, with more laughter than necessary. "Do you want another hint?"

"Yes," said Mitzi. She wanted the game over with.

"I'm made of wood," said Darwin.

Now Mitzi was certain that the so-called genius was cheating. "Nothing made of wood can fly," she accused.

"Oh yeah? How about a glider?" said Darwin. "Guess again."

"You can't be a toy plane," Mitzi told him in a schoolteacher voice, "because airplane begins with A."

"I know that," said Darwin. He dropped his chewed drumstick on the carpet and wiped his hands on his pajama bottoms.

Mitzi glared at the drumstick. She couldn't stand to touch the slobbery napkin that she had

36

used before. Finally she tore off part of the take-out box and scooped up the chicken leg with it. Where was Nana Potts, for heaven's sake? Mitzi had taken care of more than her share of Darwin's spit.

"I'm not a toy plane," Darwin continued. "I'm something big made out of wood. Give up?"

Mitzi certainly did give up. She wanted to end this boring game. "Yes," she said.

"I'm a piano," said Darwin.

A piano! Darwin was a cheater, all right. "Pianos can't fly," she informed him.

Darwin stood up and hopped back and forth. "Yes, they can. Yes, they can. Come on, I'll show you."

He raced through the living room, front hall, dining room, kitchen, and out of the back door, with Mitzi at his heels.

"So there!" he said at last, pointing.

Mitzi gasped.

Even though she had come in the front door of the house—even though she had been in a hurry —she couldn't believe that she had missed all this excitement. A moving van was parked on the street near the back door, around the corner from the front door. And a crane was parked in the driveway, closer to the house. From it, at the end of a pulley rope, hung a baby grand piano.

A workman in the crane seemed to be guiding

the piano through the open picture window of Nana Potts' bedroom by means of some levers. Two other men inside the house were reaching to grab the piano. Outside on the ground, a fourth man was watching closely.

But a lady with frizzy black hair was watching even more closely. She was waving her hands at all of them and gesturing what they should do. Dressed in bell-bottom slacks and tennis shoes, she was hopping about like a toad on a hot grill.

Who was that lady with the crazy hair? Where had Mitzi seen her before?

"Don't stand on those geraniums," yelled the lady. It was Nana Potts. Wearing someone else's hair.

Mitzi was confused. She had seen Nana Potts just before bedtime last night, wearing her regular hair. Nana Potts' regular hair was bright gold, light brown at the roots, and only medium frizzy. Unless she had dyed her hair in the middle of the night, Nana Potts was wearing a goofy wig.

"See," said Darwin righteously. "I told you pianos could fly."

"Huh?" said Mitzi. For a moment she had forgotten why Darwin had led her outside, by the new bedroom which Walter had built for Nana Potts. "What's the piano hanging on that rope for?"

"It wouldn't fit through the back hall," said

Darwin. "So they're trying to get it through the window in Nana's bedroom."

"Why don't they take it in the front door?" asked Mitzi. Everyone knew that pianos belong in living rooms.

Darwin shrugged as if Mitzi were stupid. "Because it's Nana's piano. That's why Daddy made her room so big."

So Nana Potts owned a piano. Mitzi knew all about pianos. Elsie Wolf had taught her to play two whole songs on the piano.

"Listen, lady," complained the workman standing outdoors. "A few minutes ago you were worrying because we might bang the piano. Now you're worrying about your crummy flowers. Why don't you just relax and let us do our job?"

"I'm paying you enough to move five pianos," Nana Potts answered shrilly. "The least I expect is that you treat my property with a little respect."

Darwin trotted to his grandmother's side, like a knight on horseback. "Yeah, you treat my Nana's property with a little respect!"

"Holy Moses," muttered the same workman, rolling his eyes at the clouds. "The kid's back again, too."

Like one of those cartoon animals that changes direction in midair, Nana Potts stopped scowling and smiled at Darwin. "Well, well," she said sweetly. "I see we did a good job of watching

39

for Mitzi. What did she bring us for breakfast?"

"Food," said Darwin.

"Kentucky Fried Chicken," volunteered Mitzi.

Nana Potts turned toward Mitzi. "For breakfast?" Her voice sounded strange—neither shrill nor sugary—but Mitzi felt Nana Potts was not pleased. Maybe she didn't understand the importance of Mitzi's new invention.

"Yes," explained Mitzi. "I invented it myself."

"Really?" said Nana Potts. No, she was not impressed. Mitzi was sure about that. "I hope we didn't waste all the grocery money."

"No," said Mitzi. Of course she hadn't wasted any money. She had just bought breakfast.

She was watching to see how the crane operator moved the piano to fit it through Nana Potts' window. She longed to sit on that red leather seat and work the levers that made the rope move up and down. Maybe the men would let her try it after they were through moving the piano. Maybe—

"Well, Mitzi," said Nana Potts, interrupting her thoughts. "Why don't we go upstairs now and get dressed?"

Mitzi did not care to go upstairs. She wanted to stay here where she could watch. She wanted to stay here where she could ask the men to let her have a turn with those levers after they were through. Besides, she *was* dressed. If Nana Potts wanted Darwin to get dressed, she should tell *him*.

But Mitzi didn't have a chance to say any of that out loud. Nana Potts suddenly charged after the workman she had been arguing with. "Okay, Buster," she shrieked. "I'm deducting five dollars for every geranium you ruin! That's fifteen dollars so far!"

She wasn't like a grandmother at all. Mitzi was sure that neither one of Elsie Wolf's grandmothers would yell at someone who ruined her geraniums.

Still—in a way—you had to admire a lady who told a bunch of workmen who were bigger than she was exactly what she thought.

5

The Shopping Trip

Mitzi held her chin on her hand as she sat on the back lawn. The crane that had lifted the piano into Nana Potts' bedroom was heading down the street. And Mitzi hadn't even been inside the cab.

She snatched a handful of grass and threw it angrily. She might never have another opportunity to work such an interesting machine. And all because of crabby Nana Potts, who had sent Mitzi upstairs with Darwin.

"To market, to market, to buy a fat pig—" sang Nana Potts and Darwin as they came out the back door. When she was with Darwin, Nana Potts never sounded crabby. The unfair old meany.

Scowling, Mitzi turned her head away.

"Home again, home again, jiggledy jig," continued the singers.

Mitzi refused to notice them. The song stopped.

"Well, well," said Nana Potts. "Someone doesn't want to look at us."

"Let's not take her with us," suggested Darwin.

"Where?" asked Mitzi, spinning around.

"To market, to market, to buy a fat pig," sang Darwin.

"To the grocery store," said Nana Potts, who had dressed up for the occasion. She was still wearing her frizzy wig and bell-bottom slacks. But she had put on some brown sandals and a pair of dangly gold earrings. "There's absolutely nothing in the house for me to cook," she explained.

Mitzi was pleased with that news, and she wasn't pleased. She liked going to the grocery store—if she didn't have to walk. But she didn't like the way Nana Potts kept saying there was no food in the house. Of course there was food in the house. Mitzi's mother was not Old Mother Hubbard.

Besides that insult to her mother, Nana Potts had yelled at the workmen and ruined Mitzi's whole life. Should Mitzi go to the store with someone who had done that—someone who didn't know how to act like a grandmother?

Heading toward the garage, Nana Potts called to Mitzi over her shoulder. "Are we coming?"

Mitzi sighed. She might as well go. Frederick wasn't home, and there was nothing to do. Besides, she had never ridden in Nana Potts' blue Rabbit. Next to interesting machinery and fast motorcycles, Mitzi was most interested in cars. She stood up and followed the others.

Darwin smiled sweetly at Nana Potts. "Mitzi can use my car seat. I'll sit in front with you."

Nana Potts smiled less sweetly. "Mitzi's too big for the car seat. She won't fit in it."

Of course Mitzi was too big for a car seat. She had to ride up front, where she could study all the buttons and dials.

"GRUNCH!" howled the Tyrannosaurus Rex, stamping his foot. "I'm too *tough* for a baby seat."

Mitzi ignored him and reached for the front door of the car.

"We'll get in back with Darwin and keep him company, won't we?" said Nana Potts to Mitzi. Mitzi was just about to answer no, when Nana Potts took a paper from the pocket of her pants and handed it to her. "The two of you can go over the grocery list and see if Nana has forgotten anything."

"GIMME THAT!" shouted Darwin.

Nana Potts buckled Darwin into his seat. "Mitzi can read the list aloud to us. We'll have to listen carefully, won't we?"

Mitzi liked being chosen to read aloud. As Nana Potts started the car, Mitzi cleared her throat. " 'Bak powd,' " she began.

"That means baking powder," volunteered Darwin, reading over her shoulder.

Mitzi bit her lip. She did not want to be corrected by a three-year-old.

" 'One hundred and a half all-bran,' " she continued.

"That says one hundred percent all-bran," said Darwin.

Mitzi could no longer restrain herself. "How do you know?" she asked.

"Because I can read better than you can," said Darwin, matter-of-factly.

That was too much. "Then how come I'll be in fourth grade next fall, and you haven't even started school?" Mitzi demanded.

"Because the school board doesn't know how to provide for geniuses like me. We need to elect new school board members, don't we Nana?" asked Darwin.

"You're no genius!" Mitzi cried.

Nana Potts interrupted from the front seat. "Baking powder and one hundred percent bran are two of the things I use to make bran and pecan muffins. Darwin knows that because he's helped me make them. And I told him I was going to make some for lunch," she explained. "Darwin, why don't we sit back and memorize the list while Mitzi reads it? That way we'll know if Nana has forgotten anything."

Darwin sat back in his car seat. But he wasn't memorizing anything. He was sucking his stupid finger and looking out the window.

Nevertheless, Mitzi read on. " 'Flour, brown

sugar, oranges, carrots, frozen peas, zucchini, eggs, bacon, chicken, pork chops, popcorn, cooking oil, pecans, lettuce, parsley, corn syrup, milk, butter.' "

"Well," said the voice from the front seat. "Did Nana forget anything?"

"YES!" roared the dinosaur.

"You weren't even listening," Mitzi accused.

"I was too," Darwin said. "I memorized the whole list. 'Baking powder, one hundred percent all-bran, flour, brown sugar, oranges, carrots, frozen peas, zucchini, eggs, bacon, chicken, popcorn, cooking oil, pecans, lettuce, parsley, corn syrup, milk, butter.' So there!"

"Isn't he adorable?" Nana Potts clucked. *I* couldn't repeat that list without looking."

Neither could Mitzi. But she certainly wasn't going to admit it out loud. Instead, she read silently back over the items, hoping that Darwin had made a mistake. *"You forgot pork chops! You forgot pork chops!"*

"WELL, NANA FORGOT JELLY BEANS!"

Nana Potts pulled into a parking place at the grocery store and turned off the ignition. "Shouldn't we lower our voices before we go into the store?" she asked.

Maybe, thought Mitzi. But not unless Nana Potts lowered her voice when the movers stepped on the geraniums. That was only fair.

46

"I WANT SOME JELLY BEANS!" wailed the dinosaur.

"We can't go into the store while we're yelling," Nana Potts said. "I guess we'll just have to sit in the car for a while."

Darwin leaned forward in his car seat and patted the frizzy black wig. "Nice Nana. Will you please buy me some jelly beans?"

"Nana will think about it," she replied. "If everyone else remembers to be a lady or a gentleman."

Mitzi sighed. But when would Nana Potts remember to be fair, like a real grandmother?

Inside the store, Darwin grabbed a big grocery cart. He could hardly reach the handle.

"Nana will push the cart, dear," Nana Potts suggested. "We might bump into someone."

"Mitzi and I want to be informed consumers," Darwin argued.

Consumers were people who bought things. Mitzi knew that from watching television. But she hated it when Darwin used big words. Three-year-olds shouldn't show off.

"Informed consumers need their own cart," Darwin continued.

"Well, all right," agreed Nana Potts. "The two informed consumers may shop together if Mitzi pushes the cart. Now what would we like to buy today?"

"Jelly beans," answered Darwin.

"No jelly beans until we've proved how courteous and quiet we can be in the store," said Nana Potts. She studied the grocery list which Mitzi had returned to her. "How about popcorn? Can we be informed consumers about popcorn?"

"Yes," cried Darwin.

"Yes," agreed Mitzi more softly. She guessed she could push the cart to the popcorn.

"All right then. Nana will leave you two together." Nana Potts started down the aisle.

"Which way is the popcorn?" Darwin asked Mitzi.

She didn't really know, even though she had come to this store lots of time. "I-I'm not sure."

"That's okay. I can find it," Darwin said. He raced down the aisle with Mitzi pushing the cart behind.

They tried several aisles and finally asked one of the checkers before they arrived at the popcorn display.

"Okay," challenged Darwin. "You do it."

"Do what?" asked Mitzi.

"Be an informed consumer. Choose the bag of popcorn," he explained.

Mitzi reached for a plastic bag from the shelf and set it in the cart.

"YOU DUMMY!" hooted Darwin.

A lady pushing her cart down the aisle sniffed

at Darwin and Mitzi as if they smelled bad and walked on. Mitzi had seen that woman before. Where? she wondered.

Darwin didn't seem to notice the lady's sneer. "You're not an informed consumer," he told Mitzi.

"I am so," she replied.

"You didn't read the unit prices," Darwin accused.

Mitzi quickly put the bag of popcorn back on the shelf and chose a smaller one that was cheaper.

"YOU DUMMY!" Darwin hollered again. "I KNEW YOU WEREN'T AN INFORMED CONSUMER."

Mitzi's cheeks grew hot. She felt everyone in the store was looking at her, even though the lady had moved on to the next aisle and there was no one else nearby. How dare Darwin talk to her like that. "Shh," she said.

Darwin did not care to shush. "I'VE BEEN AN INFORMED CONSUMER FOR A LONG TIME. NANA TAUGHT ME."

"Shh," Mitzi repeated more crossly. As an afterthought she added, "We have to be quiet or Nana Potts won't buy any jelly beans."

That shut Darwin up. He snapped his mouth closed like a mechanical toy. Then he leaned over to whisper. "Okay, I'll teach you." He pointed to two large bags of popcorn on the bottom shelf. "Which of those bags is cheaper?" he asked.

What a stupid question. One bag was marked $1.98. The other was marked $1.59. Anyone could see which one was cheaper. "That one," Mitzi replied, pointing.

"WRONG! YOU DIDN'T LOOK AT THE UNIT PRICES THAT TELL HOW MUCH EACH BAG COSTS A POUND. YOU'RE NOT AN INFORMED CONSUMER!" Darwin laughed so hard he fell to the floor and rolled over in merriment.

Watching him lie there, Mitzi fought a terrible urge to kick him. But two things stopped her. For one thing, she knew he would tattle to Nana Potts. For another, she realized that a woman had come down the aisle and was watching.

"Would you children please move so I can reach the popcorn?" the woman said crossly. It was the same lady who had passed them before.

Now Mitzi remembered where she had seen that lady. It was Rosie's owner, the woman who had put the sign on her gate that said BEWARE OF DOG. Once Rosie had stolen Mitzi's boot, and Mitzi had chased the dog into that yard. The lady had yelled at Mitzi and threatened to call the police.

Mitzi stepped aside, but Darwin continued to lie on the floor, laughing.

The lady glared at them. "Does your mother know where you children are?" she asked. She reached for a bag of popcorn and put it in her cart.

Mitzi hoped the lady wouldn't recognize her. "N-no," she stammered.

Darwin sprang to his feet, eager to enter the conversation. "Our daddy and mommy are on their honeymoon," he explained.

"Oh?" said the lady. Her voice was not friendly.

Mitzi gave Darwin a gentle shove. "Let's go," she whispered.

Darwin just chirped on. "Daddy and Mommy have known each other a long time, but they just decided to get married."

"Really?" said the lady. She looked at Darwin and Mitzi as if they were a pair of unwashed socks. "What's your name?"

"Charles Darwin Potts. My daddy is a biology professor—"

The lady muttered something about Charles Darwin and biologists under her breath.

Now Mitzi really did kick Darwin. But it did no good.

"—and we live at 1425 Sigsbee Avenue. Our phone number is—"

"*Come on!*" Mitzi cried, tugging his arm.

Suddenly Darwin stopped talking to the lady and turned to Mitzi. "We don't have our popcorn yet." He studied the small printing underneath all the popcorn prices on the shelves. Then he selected a bag and put it in the cart. "There. That's the one we should buy. The unit price says that by the pound that one is the cheapest." He turned to the lady again. "I'm an informed consumer. Mitzi isn't one yet, but I'm teaching her."

"Well, well, I see we found the popcorn," Nana Potts said cheerily. She had just come down the aisle pushing a huge cartful of groceries.

Rosie's owner turned to Nana Potts. "Are you the baby-sitter for these children of the—uh—biology professor?"

"Well, yes, in a way. I'm their—"

"Well," the lady interrupted. "You shouldn't bring them to the store unless you can take better care of them. They've been running and screaming like animals. And that little boy lay down on the floor so I couldn't reach the popcorn."

"You did so reach the popcorn," said Darwin, pointing to her cart. "It's right there."

The woman pinched her eyes into tight little slits. "You are the rudest child I have ever met in my life."

"Well, you're the dumbest lady I've ever met in my life," Darwin retorted. "You didn't read the unit prices any better than Mitzi. A grown-up should be an informed consumer."

"If you were my child," replied the lady, "I'd

53

spank you so hard you couldn't sit down for a week." She started off with a jerk.

Darwin whispered to his grandmother. "That lady has mean eyes, Nana. Don't you think she has mean eyes?"

"Let's go buy some jelly beans," said Nana Potts.

She bought each one of them a bag for after lunch. The biggest size.

Mitzi was almost ready to forgive Nana Potts for sending her upstairs before she could work the crane levers and for yelling at the workmen about the geraniums and for saying her mother didn't leave any food in the house. Maybe Nana Potts wanted to be a good grandmother. Maybe she just didn't know how.

But running to the check-out counter, Darwin knocked over a stack of paper towels.

"Oh dear," said Nana Potts in her sugary voice. She turned to Mitzi. "Why don't we help the stock boy pick up those towels while Darwin and Nana go through the check-out line?"

6

Mitzi's Concert

Sniff, went Mitzi as a wonderful fragrance floated upstairs from the kitchen. She set down the red crayon with which she had been drawing a new motorcycle picture and walked to the doorway for a better whiff. *Sniff, sniff.*

Ah. This was the way grandmothers were supposed to act. Grandmothers were supposed to take you with them to the grocery store. Grandmothers were supposed to buy interesting things that mothers never bothered with—pecans, baking powder, one hundred percent all-bran (whatever that was). Grandmothers were supposed to bake muffins and create nice-smelling houses like this. Yummmmmmm.

Mitzi wondered how soon lunch would be ready. Maybe she should go downstairs and find out for herself. No. Darwin was in the kitchen with Nana Potts, and Mitzi had had quite enough of Darwin for one morning.

No. Mitzi did not want to have anything to do with Darwin or his messes right now. Until lunchtime, she would find something interesting to do. Until lunchtime, she would—yes, that was it!—play Nana Potts' piano.

Wouldn't Nana Potts be pleased to discover that Mitzi could play "Chopsticks" and "Peter, Peter" all the way through?

Delighted by her wonderful idea, Mitzi skipped to the stairs and then changed her mind. She would *surprise* Nana Potts and the others by her ability to play two whole songs on the piano. That meant she should sneak to Nana Potts' bedroom while no one was watching.

Taking no chances, she looked around to make sure that Frederick was not in sight. Then, catlike, she slithered down the stairs and crept through the front hall and outdoors. Once outside, she raced to the back of the house, then stealthily reentered through the back door that led to the hall outside Nana Potts' bedroom.

From its brown face of glistening wood, the piano smiled at Mitzi with a wide row of even, white teeth. Mitzi sat down on the old-fashioned stool with the twirly seat. Too low. She stood up, spun it—*squeak*—and tried again. Too high. This time she sat on the seat while she twirled. *Sque-ak.* What fun! Nana Potts' piano seat was going to be as wonderful as her piano. *Sque-e-e-ak.*

Dizzy from so much spinning and so much excitement, Mitzi rested just a moment. Then she held out the index fingers of both hands to begin

her musical surprise. She knew she must play very
loudly so everyone could hear. So she struck the
keys very hard:

> Pe-ter, Pe-ter, pump-kin eat-er
> Had a wife and could-n't keep her,
> Put her in a pump—

"Well, well," said a voice right behind Mitzi's
back.

Mitzi almost fell off the stool. "Oooh!"

Nana Potts and Darwin were standing just inside the entrance to Nana Potts' bedroom. The
surprise had worked. Nana Potts and Darwin had
come from the kitchen to hear her music. Mitzi
smiled at them proudly.

They did not smile back.

"Mitzi was playing with only two fingers," Darwin informed his grandmother. "She wasn't playing real music."

Hmmph. Darwin was a silly three-year-old who
didn't know anything.

"That's the way you play 'Peter, Peter,'" Mitzi
told him. "With two fingers."

"You can't make real music with two fingers,"
replied Darwin. "'Peter, Peter' is just a dumb
song."

Mitzi was indignant. Of course "Peter, Peter"
was real music. What else could a song be if not
real music? Even a three-year-old should under-

stand that. But why didn't Nana Potts defend Mitzi by explaining that to Darwin?

Darwin looked up at his grandmother with big, blue eyes. "We never bang the piano, do we, Nana?"

That was too much. Mitzi had not been banging the piano. "You're just jealous because you can't play a whole song," she said.

"Yes, I can," Darwin squealed. "I'll show you." He rushed to the piano stool and gave Mitzi a shove. "Get off."

"We don't push people, do we, Darwin?" said Nana Potts.

Well. At last Nana Potts realized how awful Darwin was acting.

At last Nana Potts was doing something about Darwin, too. She walked over to the piano and shut the lid. But she turned to Mitzi as she spoke, not Darwin. "This is a very special piano that belonged to my grandmother. We never play it without permission."

Mitzi climbed off the stool and stared at her shoes, which looked clunky next to Darwin's little pink toes. She had the feeling that Nana Potts expected her to say she was sorry for something. But Mitzi was not sorry. She had just wanted to surprise everyone by playing a whole song on the piano. Why should she be sorry about that?

"And we never go into other people's rooms without asking permission," continued Nana

Potts. She was trying still harder to make Mitzi sorry.

Well, Mitzi would never be sorry. This was *her* house. Nana Potts should be sorry for moving into it without Mitzi's permission. And for taking the best bedroom that Mitzi herself wanted. So there!

"No, we never go into other people's rooms without asking permission," repeated the little poll parrot.

How dare Darwin talk that way! Why this very morning he had come into Mitzi's room without asking permission. *And he had jumped on Mitzi's stomach!*

Mitzi wanted to turn and run, but her big, clunky feet felt like steel weights on the carpet. She wanted to say something terrible to Darwin. But she couldn't think of anything mean enough. Her tongue felt like a steel weight, too.

"Well," said Nana Potts with a fakey smile. "I'm sure we'll be more careful next time. I'm sure we'll knock on the door and ask for permission before we play the piano."

"And we won't bang it," suggested Darwin.

"You mean *you* won't bang it," retorted Mitzi. "I never bang pianos. And my name isn't *we.* It's *Mitzi.*" Mitzi smiled inwardly. She had put the little show-off in his place.

Nana Potts didn't notice Mitzi's clever reply. "And we'll never play the piano again with dirty hands, will we?" she said. "Now let's go wash our hands. Lunch is ready."

That was the last straw. Mitzi's hands were not dirty. She would not wash them. No one could make her.

"No!" Mitzi howled.

"Oooh," gasped Nana Potts.

Mitzi felt pleased. She had shocked Nana Potts. But deep down, she felt a little worried, too. Maybe she wasn't being polite. Maybe she was even acting as awful as Darwin did. But her voice wouldn't stop yelling.

"I don't want to wash my hands!" hollered Mitzi. "I'm not hungry!" she lied.

Nana Potts seemed unable to speak.

But Darwin filled the silence. "Mitzi's having a temper tantrum," he observed. "Shame on Mitzi."

"Rrr," growled Mitzi under her breath, unable to put her feelings into real words. She spun around and headed toward her room, the shortest way possible.

Unfortunately, the shortest route to her room took her through the kitchen. There Frederick was standing openmouthed. He had heard the whole quarrel. Also, in the kitchen the warm smell of freshly baked muffins reminded Mitzi that she was very hungry. Well, she would show Nana Potts. She would show everybody. She would

60

never eat again until they all said they were sorry.

She raced to her room, slammed the door, threw herself facedown on the bedspread, and planned how she would make everyone miserable. They would be sorry when she didn't eat. They would be sorry when she got sick. Poor Mitzi, they would say. Hungry and sick and dying. All because of *them*.

And what about Mitzi's mother? How would she feel when she came home and found her poor Mitzi dying from lack of food? Sorry. That's how she'd feel. Sorry for getting married. Sorry for going on a honeymoon without Mitzi. Sorry for leaving Mitzi home with these crazy people.

Mitzi pictured how sad her mother would look, bending over sick Mitzi's bed. Thinking about the unhappy scene, Mitzi wanted to cry. But no tears would come.

New bready smells wafted upstairs, through the open window, under the door of Mitzi's room. She rolled over and lay on her back. Was Nana Potts baking them another batch of muffins? There were noises, too. The tinkle of glasses. Dim conversation.

Mitzi was shocked. They were eating their lunch and talking, as if nothing had happened.

This wasn't the way she had planned it. No one cared that poor Mitzi wasn't at the lunch table with them. No one cared that poor Mitzi was upstairs starving to death. They were eating their warm muffins and talking as if nothing else mattered.

Poor, poor Mitzi.

Bending her elbow, Mitzi propped her head on one hand to listen. Were they talking about her? Maybe. Maybe not. The voices were too muffled to tell.

Quietly she stood up, tiptoed to the door, and opened it a crack. She heard Frederick saying something and then Darwin squealing. But the words were not clear.

Only the smell of warm muffins was clear. Mitzi's stomach growled. Should she wash her hands and go downstairs? No. Never. She would starve to death first.

Mitzi heard footsteps downstairs. Someone was coming her way. Quickly she shut her door and fell back on her bed. Up the stairs came the footsteps. Mitzi lay still, afraid to breathe.

Knock, knock. It sounded like kicking on the door.

Mitzi didn't answer. Let them think she was too weak.

Knock, knock, knock. More kicking. And louder this time.

At least Nana Potts, or whoever it was, wasn't barging in Mitzi's room without permission.

"Hey, Mitzi. It's me, Frederick. Open up. This tray can't exactly fly by its own power, you know."

Well, she wasn't mad at Frederick, so much. He hadn't really done anything but listen. And maybe he was bringing some of those muffins on his tray. "Come in," she said hoarsely.

"You'll have to open the door for me. Room service was fresh out of carts, and my hands are busy."

Mitzi opened the door slowly.

Frederick set the tray on her desk with a windy sigh. "Lunch gets heavier every year. They don't make calories the way they used to."

Mitzi paid no attention to what he was talking about. She was staring at the food on the tray—two bran and pecan muffins spread with butter, a small glass of milk, carrot and pineapple salad garnished with a curlicue of orange and a sprig of parsley.

She felt her saliva sloshing and wished Frederick would leave the room. It hardly seemed right to eat in front of anyone when she was supposed to be starving to death.

Frederick seemed to know what she was thinking. "Go on, eat it," he said with a shrug. "It's no ice out of my Coke if your hands are clean or not."

Mitzi understood *part* of that. The important part. She sat on her desk chair. Then she grabbed a muffin with one "dirty" hand and bit off a mouthful. Yummmm. It was still warm. And more heavenly tasting than she'd dreamed. She swallowed the first mouthful and took another.

63

But why didn't Frederick leave? Mitzi still felt uncomfortable about eating in front of anyone.

Frederick had no intention of leaving. He settled himself on the edge of her bed.

"Darwin and I didn't get those curly orange things on our plates," Frederick said.

Well. Mitzi studied the curlicue more closely— a thin slice of orange cut partway through and then twisted. She liked it even better than she had at first.

Frederick lay back on Mitzi's bed, resting his head on clasped hands. She could see the crooked part in his dark brown hair. "Nana means well," he said. "You'll just have to be patient with her."

Patient? What a strange idea! "Children aren't supposed to be patient with grown-ups," she informed him. "Grown-ups are supposed to be patient with children."

Frederick sighed. He took off his glasses and squinted at them, as if they were very interesting. "That's the popular conception, all right, but I've observed it to be false."

"Huh?" said Mitzi.

"Well," said Nana Potts, who suddenly appeared out of the air. She had removed her wig, and her regular hair looked even worse than usual —all matted down and straggly. "I hope we enjoyed our lunch."

Mitzi felt generous. And patient. "Yes. It was very good. Thank you."

Frederick pointed to Mitzi with an elbow. "I told her this morning about some of your other specialties, like peanut butter popcorn balls. Greg is coming over to play chess this afternoon. He loves your peanut butter popcorn balls."

Nana Potts gave Frederick a sugary smile. "Not as much as you do, though. But flattery won't work. I have an appointment to go to the beauty parlor for a touch-up so I won't have to wear that wig. June is no month for wigs. My head felt as hot as a firecracker."

"You can't go off and leave Greg and me with Darwin," argued Frederick. "He always ruins our games!"

Nana pinched up her lips, thinking. Then she turned to Mitzi. "I'm sure we won't mind watching Darwin while I'm gone, will we?"

Yes! Yes! We *would* mind watching Darwin. Mitzi had been doing it all day.

She nearly screamed it out loud, but she was distracted by something else. Someone was playing a tune on the piano—a much more difficult tune than the songs Mitzi knew.

Frederick and Nana Potts were both here in Mitzi's room with her.

It was Darwin. The dumb three-year-old genius was playing Nana Potts' piano. With all his dirty fingers.

7

The Game Plan

"This is Greg Walker," Frederick explained after letting his friend inside the door. "And this is my stepsister, Mitzi McAllister."

Greg shrugged and waved two fingers more or less in Mitzi's direction. He was as tall as a grownup, but certainly didn't have grown-up manners.

"Hello," said Mitzi, polite nonetheless.

Without answering, Greg stuffed his big fists in his pockets and studied the front hall. You could tell he was more interested in the new house Frederick had moved to than in any new stepsisters he might have.

As usual, Frederick's voice filled the silence. "Her name is McAllister now, but as soon as my father adopts her, she'll change her name to Potts like the rest of us. Mitzi Potts."

Change her name to Potts? How dare Frederick tell Greg a thing like that! Mitzi McAllister was her very own name that had belonged to her since she was a little girl. Of course she wouldn't change it. She considered telling Frederick he was

67

a big fibber, but decided to postpone it. She wasn't likely to win an argument against *two* eleven-year-old boys, one of whom was nearly tall enough to be her father. She'd wait to tell Frederick until Greg went home. Besides, she was trying to figure out something else right now.

Why were Frederick Potts and Greg Walker friends? That was what she was trying to figure out. They didn't seem at all alike. For one thing, Frederick's head didn't even reach Greg's chin. (Was Frederick the sort of person who would choose a friend he had to look up to?) For another, Greg wasn't exactly talkative. (But maybe that was why Frederick liked him.) For another, Greg never looked you in the eye the way Frederick did. In fact, the way he kept his hands buried in his pockets and his shoulders hunkered over, you had the feeling he was trying to disappear.

But Greg did have one thing in common with Frederick. He wore messages. His lavender T-shirt said, IF YOU DRINK, DON'T DRIVE.

Lavender, which was not Mitzi's favorite color, looked especially yucky next to Greg's thick hair, which was the color of tomato sauce. Even so, Mitzi decided that Greg's face was sort of nice. With tomato sauce hair, mozzarella skin, and big round freckles, it reminded her of pepperoni pizza.

"Didn't you bring your chess set?" Frederick asked.

Greg shook his head. "We can use yours."

"No, we can't," Frederick said. "I told you. My father took it on his honeymoon. He wants to teach Patricia how to play."

Greg giggled. For such a big person, he had a silly laugh. "I thought you were kidding."

"Of course I wasn't kidding. Why would I be kidding?" said Frederick in a voice that sounded angry. Were these friends quarreling?

"No one," boomed Greg, who had a loud voice after all, "plays chess on a honeymoon."

Yes, they were quarreling. Frederick's voice was booming, too. "Why not? Tell me one reason why not."

"Well—" Greg began. Had his pizza face changed color? Yes. It seemed overbaked. "Most people—do something more romantic. Most people—at least go dancing."

Now the quarrel was about Mitzi's mother and stepfather. She felt she should stick up for them. But she didn't know what to say.

Luckily Frederick was never at a loss for words. "My parents don't like to dance. My parents are intellectuals."

Mitzi had never heard Frederick call her mother anything but Patricia. It sounded nice when he said "my parents."

Greg twisted the sole of his Nike on the parquet floor. "Okay, okay, you don't need to take it personally," he said.

Hah! Frederick had won! Mitzi was proud about that.

Greg shrugged again. "I didn't want to play chess anyway. Let's play Battleship."

"I don't play Battleship anymore," Frederick said.

"How come?" Greg demanded.

Frederick sewed up his lips thoughtfully, pausing before he spoke. "It's too aggressive. I've sworn off aggressive games. Maybe if people didn't play aggressive games when they were young, they wouldn't grow up to start wars. Maybe—"

"Oh, gimme a break," Greg moaned.

"Let's play Scrabble," Frederick suggested.

"You always win at Scrabble," said Greg. "You know I can't play word games."

"Let's play Monopoly," said Darwin, who had *smack-smack*ed into the front hall wearing blue swim fins. Apparently he was tired of being a flying piano because he had put on his familiar tyrannosaurus rex feet.

"Yes, let's play Monopoly," agreed Mitzi. She hoped she would be the first to land on Boardwalk and Park Place.

"Okay, I'll play Monopoly," Frederick said to

Greg, as if Greg had been the one to suggest it.

"I get to use the car," said Tyrannosaurus Rex.

Mitzi sighed. She had wanted to use the car herself.

Greg scowled in the direction of Mitzi and Darwin. "Do they have to play too?"

"Oh no," said Frederick. "Mitzi promised to keep Darwin out of our way."

Mitzi had not promised! "I did not," she said.

"I want to play Monopoly," Darwin insisted.

"No," said Frederick. "You always wrinkle the money."

"I do not!" exclaimed Darwin. "I'm going to play." He stuck his left index finger in his mouth and sucked defiantly.

Mitzi smiled to herself. For once she was enjoying the Tyrannosaurus Rex's awful behavior. Maybe if he acted stubborn enough, Frederick would let both of them play.

"Plus you always get your disgusting slobber on the dice," Frederick added. "You're always sucking your stupid finger."

Darwin removed his finger from his mouth with a *plop*! A spray of saliva caught Greg on the arm. "I am not!" Darwin argued.

Greg rubbed his arm against his anti-drunk driving T-shirt and turned to Mitzi. "Why don't you help that kid dissolve?"

Mitzi considered that suggestion. How could you help someone dissolve? she wondered. Ice dissolved. Smoke dissolved. But there was no way that she could help Darwin dissolve. Greg must not be very smart—not at all like Frederick or the other people in her family.

"People don't dissolve," she told him.

Greg responded to the information with a sneer. "You nerd," he said. "Take Darwin and get lost."

"Hey, lay off my sister!" Frederick said.

Well. Frederick had not just defended their parents against Greg. He had defended Mitzi, too. She liked that. She especially liked the way he said "my sister."

Maybe, when she landed on Boardwalk and Park Place, she would trade one of them to Frederick for all the green or yellow streets. She wanted to show him that she was on his side. If they teamed up together, they could beat a dummy like Greg Walker.

Frederick looked at Mitzi. "I'll make you a bargain," he said. "If you'll keep Darwin out of our way today, I'll watch him the next time one of your friends comes over."

Mitzi chewed her lip. Frederick had a point, all right. Up to now, she and Elsie Wolf had always tried to play at Mitzi's house because of Elsie's babyish little sister, who never paid attention to anything you told her. Now at Mitzi's house there was the terrible Tyrannosaurus Rex.

Mitzi thought about how Darwin had pounced

on her stomach early this morning, playing dinosaur. She thought about the way he had nearly fallen from the ceiling later on, playing flying piano. She wondered about the new kinds of mischief he would stir up from now on, whenever Elsie came over to play. That would be soon, too. Any day now, Elsie would be home from her vacation. It would be nice to have Frederick keep Darwin out of their way.

Still, the thought of spending the rest of the afternoon alone with Darwin the Dinosaur was almost more than she could bear.

"If you'll let Darwin and me play Monopoly with you, I'll give you my bag of jelly beans," Mitzi offered.

Greg made a face. "I hate jelly beans."

"So does Frederick," Darwin whispered. "That's why I always ask Nana to buy them."

"Did your grandmother make us any peanut butter popcorn?" Greg asked.

"No," answered Frederick with a sigh. "She didn't have time. She had an appointment."

Mitzi sighed, too. It seemed to her that Nana Potts always had an appointment.

8

Mr. Hathaway

"This is the lab where I'm going to invent a bionic brain. This is the lab where I'm going to invent talking trees. This is the lab where I'm going to invent the Charles Darwin Potts Ninth Symphony and Chorus." Surrounded by Lego toys and jelly beans, the dumb genius was sitting cross-legged on the front porch and talking to himself.

The front porch had seemed like the best place to baby-sit Darwin. It was pretty far from the living room. The Tyrannosaurus Rex couldn't climb all over the Monopoly board and slobber on the dice. But it was also pretty close. If Frederick changed his mind about inviting Mitzi to play, she would be sure to hear him call.

Darwin had built something he called the Charles Darwin Potts Research Park. It had taken Mitzi three trips to bring enough Lego toys from his room upstairs. But at the time, she thought it would be worth the effort. The more things Darwin had to keep himself busy, the longer he would stay out of her hair.

Unfortunately, Mitzi had made a mistake. The flies on the porch were driving her crazy. And she had brought so much stuff out (including her own card table and chair) that she didn't have the energy to take it all inside again.

Mitzi blew her bangs out of her eyes. Her drawing of a crane lifting a baby grand piano was not going well. She knew there had been only two wheels under the cab of the crane this morning. But she couldn't remember how many wheels there had been in the part behind the cab.

One of the reasons she had chosen to work on the porch was in hopes another crane might drive by for her to study. So far, however, nothing more interesting than a jeep full of teenagers had passed the house.

Another very important reason was so that Nana Potts would see her as soon as she drove home. As long as Mitzi was going to baby-sit Darwin, it was only right that people should notice.

"This is the lab where I'm going to invent a nuclear bomb for insects," Darwin muttered. "It won't kill anything else, but it will get rid of all the bugs in the world."

The flies seemed to be getting to him, too.

Suddenly Mitzi had an idea. She ran into the house and returned with a fly swatter.

"Play that this is an insect bomb," she suggested. "See how many flies you can get."

Pleased with herself, Mitzi sat down again at the card table. Should she color the cab red or yellow?

WHOP went something painful on Mitzi's back. She turned around and saw Darwin grinning at her.

"You're dead, you big fly!" Darwin cried.

"Darwin!" she shrieked as he raised his arm to strike her again. "I'm not a fly!"

"Yes, you are. You're a big, mean, giant fly. I don't kill poor little flies. I only kill big mean giant ones."

"Give me that fly swatter," Mitzi ordered, grabbing it.

Before she could hit him, Darwin ducked out of reach. "Catch me," he challenged and darted down the steps.

Mitzi sprang from her chair. "Ouch!" she cried as she slipped on a Lego toy and fell. By the time she stood up again, Darwin had a good head start. She raced down the steps after him.

Darwin could not run very fast, but he zigzagged back and forth, trying to fool her. She was so eager to catch him and give *him* a whop with the fly swatter that Mitzi saw nothing else. She ran smack into a man who had been walking up and down the street ringing doorbells.

"Oof," grunted Mitzi. "I'm, sorry."

She looked up, expecting to be scolded, but the

man was smiling. "Are you kids practicing for the hockey team or something?"

The man had gray hair and nice wrinkles around his eyes. Those things, as well as the overalls he was wearing, reminded Mitzi of the helpful janitor at her school, Mr. Ledgard. So she liked the man at once.

"Darwin hit me, so I was trying to hit him back," Mitzi explained sheepishly. Maybe this nice man wouldn't like her if he thought she went around picking on little kids.

Darwin charged over. "I'm Charles Darwin Potts," he began. "My daddy is a biology professor—"

Why did Darwin always interrupt? Mitzi considered saying, "My mother is an archaeology professor," but Darwin didn't give her a chance.

"We live at 1425 Sigsbee Avenue," Darwin rattled on. "Our phone number is 581–6272. I'm three years and four months old. I'm an informed consumer, and I invent bionic brains."

"Well, that's pretty heady stuff," said the man, making a joke. "Your father wouldn't be Walter Potts, would he?"

"How did you know?" squealed Darwin. "Do you know Daddy?"

"I went on picnics with him all the time when he was a little boy," said the man. "I have a son the same age, and they used to play together.

Your grandparents were pretty good friends of ours a long time ago. Before your grandfather and my wife died."

"You know Nana?" Darwin exclaimed.

"Mary Beth Potts is the best cook I ever met. Her lemon pie would tame a wolf." The man closed his eyes as if he were dreaming about taming wolves with lemon pie.

"Have you ever tasted her peanut butter popcorn balls?" Darwin asked.

Mitzi scowled. This man was her friend, not Darwin's. Why couldn't Darwin keep still?

"I can't say that I have," said the man, awake again.

"She makes the best peanut butter popcorn balls in the whole world," said Darwin. "I'll tell her to invite you over the next time she makes some."

"Thank you," said the man. The smile crinkles around his eyes deepened.

Mitzi hated being left out. "Nana Potts is my grandma now, too," she felt obliged to say.

"Mommy and Daddy were married yesterday," explained Darwin. "They're on their honeymoon."

"Good for them!" said the man. "Well, I guess they won't be needing my services for a while. Here, I'll leave you one of my business cards anyway. You can give it to your daddy when he gets home."

Mitzi must have looked disappointed because he gave her a small green card, too. "And you can give one to your mother," he said.

"Thank you," said Mitzi, studying the black letters:

HATHAWAY AND HATHAWAY TREE EXPERTS
We specialize in tough jobs.
Topping, Trimming, Cabling, Feeding, Spraying
Milo Hathaway   1327 East Oaks Drive   945–6330

"Are you Mr. Hathaway and Hathaway?" asked Darwin.

"I'm one Mr. Hathaway. Milo," said the man. "I'm in business with my son Bob. He has business cards too, with his name on them."

"When I go into the biology business with my father, we'll have business cards that say Potts and Potts," said Darwin. "My card will say Charles Darwin Potts."

"Good idea," agreed Mr. Hathaway. "Well, the next time you see your grandma, tell her hello for Milo Hathaway."

"I'll tell her today, as soon as she comes home," said Darwin.

"Is she baby-sitting while your daddy is on his honeymoon?"

"Nana Potts lives with us," explained Mitzi, who felt ignored.

"I'll tell her to make us some lemon pie and peanut butter popcorn balls," said Darwin.

"All *right*!" said Mr. Hathaway.

Mitzi giggled. It seemed funny to hear a man with gray hair talking like a teenager.

"Hey, Dad" called a voice from the road.

Mitzi spun around to see something very exciting. Parked in front of her house was *a truck with a crane!* It was smaller than the crane that had lifted Nana Potts' piano this morning. And it had a cage at the end of the arm instead of a hook. But nevertheless it was *a crane!*

"Is that your crane?" Mitzi asked Mr. Hathaway.

"You mean that cherry picker?" said Mr. Hathaway. "Yes, that's ours."

"Does that truck pick cherries?" asked Darwin.

"No, it's called a cherry picker because some people use trucks like that when they pick cherries," said Mr. Hathaway. "That cage goes up and down like an elevator, and people ride in it to reach the tall limbs of cherry trees."

Mitzi gasped. The thoughts of working the controls to make a crane move a piano were exciting enough. But riding up and down in a cage like that was the most wonderful thing she could think of.

Darwin was reading Mr. Hathaway's business card. "This doesn't say you pick cherries. Why don't you tell people you pick cherries?"

"Dad," called the man in the truck, "we've got to go. A lady around the corner is waiting for us. She has a job she wants done right away.

"Yeah?" said Mr. Hathaway. "Well, there's a trimming job across the street we can do afterward, if there's time."

"Why don't you tell people you pick cherries?" Darwin demanded.

"That card is too small to list all the things Bob and I do to trees. But we don't usually pick cherries," said Mr. Hathaway.

"Dad!" urged his son.

"I want to ride up and down in your cherry picker elevator," said Darwin.

"I tell you what," said Mr. Hathaway with a wink. "You get your grandma to make us some lemon pie and peanut butter popcorn, and I'll give you the best ride you've ever had." He climbed in the truck beside his son and waved as they drove off.

9

The Jelly Bean Mystery

At her card table on the front porch, Mitzi held up the picture of the cherry picker she had just drawn. It was good. *Very* good. Maybe she would even give it to Mr. Hathaway. Maybe Mr. Hathaway would even frame it, the way Mr. Ledgard, the janitor at her school, had framed the picture of the motorcycle she had once made for him.

Darwin had moved to the far end of the porch, where he was drawing something he didn't want Mitzi to see. As soon as Mr. Hathaway left, Darwin had asked Mitzi for some papers and felt-tip pens. She didn't mind sharing. She had plenty of both. Besides, drawing had kept Darwin quiet for a long time.

In fact, Darwin had been so quiet she almost worried about him. Now and then she had looked across the porch, just to make sure he was still there. He had spilled his jelly beans, picking them up from the dirty floor to eat them as he drew. But Mitzi didn't scold. Anything to keep him still.

From the living room, where Frederick and

Greg were playing Monopoly, came wild laughter. Someone must have landed on Boardwalk or received two hundred dollars from the Community Chest. Who cared? Mitzi was glad those mean boys hadn't invited her to play. If she were playing Monopoly indoors, she would never have seen the cherry picker. If she were playing Monopoly indoors, she would never have met Mr. Hathaway. So there!

Darwin stood up and toddled over to the card table. "See my business card?" he said. He handed Mitzi a large sheet of paper, scrawled with big, uneven letters:

POTTS AND POTTS BIOLOGY INVENSHUNS
WE DO HARD THINGS   CHARLES DARWIN
POTTS   1425 SIXBY AVNUE   581–6272

"Why Darwin," Mitzi exclaimed. "That's very good." She meant it, too. Not many three-year-olds could print and spell that well.

Darwin burrowed for a red jelly bean from Mitzi's plastic bag on the card table. Then he ran back to the corner of the porch and brought back another piece of paper. "I made you one, too," he mumbled as he chewed.

POTTS AND POTTS DRAWINGS
WE DO HARD PICKSTURES   MITZI
POTTS   1425 SICKSBY AVUNE   58
1–6272

"Thank you," she said, wondering if she should tell him that her name wasn't Potts. Her name was McAllister. She would always be Mitzi McAllister. But then she remembered how bad she had felt, long ago, when her mother hadn't liked the motorcycle pictures Mitzi had made for her and didn't hang them on the walls.

Anyway, Darwin had been very sweet to make the business card for Mitzi. Sometimes he was really cute.

"That's the nicest present I've ever received," she lied. "I'm going to hang it in my bedroom."

Darwin grinned and picked up Mitzi's bag of jelly beans to burrow for another red candy.

Br—r-ring! went the telephone. *Br—r-ring!*

"I'll get it!" Darwin squealed. He dropped the bag of jelly beans with a clatter and raced to the door.

Darwin would *not* answer Mitzi's telephone! He never delivered messages or called the right people to the phone. Mitzi would answer it herself. She dropped the calling card Darwin had made for her on the table, on top of the jelly bean bag. Then she chased after him.

Br—r-ring! Br—r-ring! Br—r-ring!

Darwin reached the receiver in the kitchen first. "Hello," he said brightly. "Potts' residence."

It was not Potts' residence. It was McAllisters' residence. This was Mitzi's house.

86

"Charles Darwin Potts speaking," Darwin chattered on. "Do you need any biology inventions?"

There was a pause while the person on the other end answered.

"I bet you need a bionic brain," Darwin chirped.

Mitzi grabbed the receiver from his hand. "Hello," she said as Darwin wandered off and left the room.

"Hi," said Elsie Wolf. "Who's the dingbat? I thought I had the wrong number."

"Oh, that's just the dinosaur genius," Mitzi replied. "I told you about him. When did you get back from your vacation?"

"A little while ago," said Elsie. "I brought you a shell necklace from the gift shop at the beach."

"Thank you," said Mitzi politely, even though she didn't need a shell necklace from the beach. Why hadn't Elsie bought her a miniature motorcycle for her collection?

"Can you come over and get it?" Elsie asked.

"Uh—not today," Mitzi stammered. "I have to watch Darwin while Frederick's friend is here. Can you come over?"

"Not now," said Elsie. "Dad and Mother are taking a nap and I have to baby-sit Janna Lee."

There was silence on the line while Mitzi wondered what to say. Was this what her life would be like from now on—never able to play with Elsie because of troublesome Janna Lee and the terrible Tyrannosaurus Rex?

"How about coming over tomorrow?" suggested Elsie. "We can play with my new Glamour Gal dolls. They're littler than Barbie dolls. Just the right size for your motorcycles. You can bring some of your motorcycles with you."

Mitzi thought about that. She thought about how Elsie's little sister always cried to play with Elsie's toys and then spilled honey and jam all over them. She did not want honey and jam on her motorcycles.

From the living room came Frederick's excited laughter, and Mitzi got a wonderful idea.

"Why don't you come over here tomorrow?" she suggested. "We can play Monopoly. Frederick promised to keep Darwin out of my way the next time I have a friend over."

Mitzi felt a tug on her leg. Darwin had come back. "I don't want Frederick to watch me," he said. "I want to play Monopoly with you."

"No," Mitzi told him in her schoolteacher voice. "It's your turn to play with Frederick tomorrow."

Darwin patted her arm. "Nice sister. I like you better."

Hmmph. Well, Mitzi wasn't going to fall for that trick again. "That's nice. I like you, too. But tomorrow you're going to play with Frederick."

"I like you even if you did let a monster bomb my research park," Darwin continued. "I like you even if you did let a monster steal all the jelly beans."

"Mitzi?" said Elsie. Her voice sounded funny because Mitzi had taken the receiver away from her ear. "Are you still there?"

"Yes, I'm here," Mitzi said into the phone. "Just a minute." She turned to Darwin. "There are no such things as monsters. Monsters are make-believe."

"Yes, there are so monsters," argued Darwin. "I saw him. He turned the card table upside down and ate all the jelly beans except this one." He held up a hand covered with black goo.

Mitzi sighed with irritation. "I'll be there in a minute. You go wash your hands."

"I'm sorry, Elsie," Mitzi said into the mouthpiece. "Darwin never leaves me alone for a minute."

"I know how you feel," said Elsie. "Since we've been back from our vacation, Janna Lee has put one of my Glamour Gal dolls in the dishwasher and torn Dad's new magazine."

"Well, can you come over tomorrow?" Mitzi urged.

"Ooh!" wailed Elsie. "Janna Lee is washing some dishes in the toilet. I've got to go." She slammed the receiver.

Mitzi sat by the phone for a minute, wondering if Elsie would call her back.

From the living room came more laughter.

"Oh, Darwin!" howled Frederick.

What was Darwin doing in the living room? Mitzi thought he had gone into the bathroom to wash his hands.

"YOU LOOK JUST LIKE HER!" Greg howled.

Was Darwin mimicking Mitzi? He better not be!

Footsteps stormed through the dining room and down the new hall Walter had built to Nana Potts' bedroom. Someone banged the piano keys.

They *were* making fun of her!

Piano music, Darwin's squeaky singing, and more laughter came from Nana Potts' bedroom.

Should she find out what they were doing? Yes. She would spy on them.

Softly Mitzi tiptoed through the kitchen and down the hallway, far enough to see inside the open door of Nana Potts' room.

Long, dangly earrings wobbled on Darwin's ears as he swayed back and forth on the piano stool. A frizzy black wig fell nearly to his eyes. He wasn't mimicking Mitzi. He was mimicking Nana Potts. Even Mitzi couldn't help smiling as she watched.

Just as quietly as she had come, Mitzi sneaked off. Then she went to the porch to see what had happened to her jelly beans.

Never had Mitzi seen a bigger mess. Never. The card table was upside down. The chair was turned on its side. Lego toys, felt-tip pens, and pieces of paper were strewn all over the porch—like confetti on New Year's Eve. How dare Darwin make a mess like this and blame it on a make-believe monster!

Well. Mitzi hadn't made this mess. And she wasn't going to clean it up. So there!

Suddenly Mitzi realized that the cherry picker was parked across the street. Standing in the cage, Mr. Hathaway was being hoisted to a tall tree. How wonderful to ride in a cage like that—your own private elevator.

Just then Nana Potts' blue Rabbit turned the corner and headed toward home. Her car passed the truck, skidded to a stop, and then backed up.

Nana Potts stuck her head out the car window. Her hair was no longer bright gold with light brown at the roots. It was no longer frizzy black. It was as orange as a Halloween pumpkin.

"Milo Hathaway," called Nana Potts. "Is that you?"

"Mary Beth Potts," he replied. "Is that you?"

Mitzi sat down on the porch steps and watched while Nana Potts and Mr. Hathaway chatted. She wished Mr. Hathaway would tell Nana Potts to bring Mitzi across the street to ride in his cage. Should she go over there herself and join the conversation?

Yipes. A terrible thought struck her. What if Nana Potts should go into her bedroom and find Darwin mimicking her and the other boys laughing? Mitzi better go warn them.

She stood up and rushed toward the house. In her haste she tripped over a Lego toy in the front hall. Ouch! she thought, rubbing her knee. That's the second time she had stumbled over one of those dumb blocks. Everything had gone wrong today. And it was all Darwin's and Nana Potts' fault. At last she stood up and hurried to Nana Potts' bedroom.

Too late. Nana Potts was already in the bedroom, watching Darwin play the piano.

At first Mitzi thought that Nana Potts was shaking with rage. No. She was laughing. Harder than the others.

Nana Potts finally caught her breath long enough to speak. "Isn't he adorable?" she gasped.

Mitzi was not relieved.

How come Nana Potts hadn't noticed that Darwin's hands were covered with yuck? How come Nana Potts had scolded Mitzi when *she* played the piano? How come Nana Potts hadn't said, "Isn't Mitzi adorable?"

10

A Picnic With Nana Potts

It was not possible to keep secrets from Nana Potts. Despite her thick glasses (or maybe because of them), she could see everywhere. She discovered the torn paper and Lego toys on the front porch before Mitzi had a chance to make Darwin clean the mess up.

The old busybody.

Nana Potts changed back into her wide-bottom slacks and insisted that everyone help her clean the porch up. She didn't actually *say* the mess was Mitzi's fault for not watching Darwin closer. But that's what she was thinking. And because Nana Potts thought it, so did everyone else. No one spoke to Mitzi the whole time they worked.

Even after the porch was neat again, a cloud of gloom hung over all their heads.

Nana Potts was angry about finding the porch in such a mess. She went into the kitchen, still looking ready to explode.

Greg was angry about losing at Monopoly and

about the lack of treats at Mitzi's house. He left to go home and find something to eat.

Frederick was angry about being expected to help clean up the porch. He packed his clothes (and his Scrabble game) to spend the night at Greg's.

Mitzi was angry about being treated as if everything were her fault. She had done nothing wrong. She had only tried to help. And no one appreciated her. She withdrew to the dining room with a motorcycle magazine. She would not go into the kitchen with Nana Potts and Darwin. Not even if they begged her.

Only Darwin, who had caused all the problems, remained smiling and chatty. From the dining room table, where she was looking at the pictures in her magazine, Mitzi could hear his cheerful conversation.

"A lady is coming up the sidewalk, Nana," Darwin informed his grandmother.

Squeak went the cupboard door as it opened.

"She's coming up the driveway to our house," Darwin reported.

Clang went a glass bowl on the kitchen counter.

"It's the lady with the mean eyes," said Darwin. "The old witch who yelled at me in the grocery store."

Bam went the cupboard door as it shut.

Knock, knock, knock went a noise on the door.

95

"She's knocking on the door, Nana," said Darwin.

"I hear her," said Nana Potts.

"Aren't you going to open the door?" asked Darwin.

"I don't feel like talking to anyone right now," said Nana Potts. "Especially her."

CRASH! went the door.

Mitzi jumped up. Despite her vow not to go into the kitchen, she couldn't resist peeking. The lady had knocked the door open, without being invited!

"I heard what you said!" cried Rosie's owner. "Why didn't you open the door?"

"I've had a bad day," said Nana Potts. "And you haven't helped things."

"Well, I've had a bad day, too," said the woman. "And it's all the fault of these children you're supposed to be watching."

"Mitzi and I didn't do anything to you," Darwin said.

The lady looked down at Darwin with her mean eyes. "I guess it's not your fault that Rosie has been vomiting all over my new carpet," the lady said sarcastically.

"Who's Rosie?" Darwin asked.

"As soon as I saw that Rosie was sick, I knew these wicked children had been feeding her something. Jelly beans! That's what they fed her. She vomited jelly beans all over my new carpet!" the woman screamed. "She could have choked on jelly beans. She could have died."

"I don't know Rosie," said Darwin. "Who's Rosie?"

The lady ignored him. "Well, you can't pretend these children aren't responsible," she said to Nana Potts. "I have proof. Listen to this: 'Potts and Potts Drawings. We do hard pictures. Mitzi Potts. 1425 Sigsbee Avenue. 581–6272.' " She thrust a wrinkled paper in Nana Potts' face.

It was the business card Darwin had made for Mitzi. But how did the lady get it? she wondered.

"So?" said Nana Potts.

Mitzi gasped. Her mother never allowed Mitzi to say "so." Yet here was Nana Potts—a grown-up lady—saying "so" to another grown-up.

"I don't know any girls named Rosie," Darwin insisted.

"Rosie is a dog," said Mitzi. "She lives in the corner house on University Street."

"AHA!" said the woman, turning toward the doorway where Mitzi stood. "I knew you were the one who poisoned my dog."

"I didn't poison your dog," said Mitzi. "I like Rosie. Sometimes."

"Is Rosie a black dog?" asked Darwin.

"Yes," said Mitzi.

"With brown ears?" Darwin wanted to know.

"Yes," said Mitzi.

Darwin tugged on the lady's skirt. "Rosie is a

bad dog. She bombed my Charles Darwin Potts Research Park and stole all the jelly beans. She knocked Lego toys and paper all over our porch."

All of a sudden Nana Potts was interested in this conversation. "You mean it was a *dog* who made that mess?" she asked Darwin.

"Yes," said Darwin.

"Why didn't you tell me?"

Darwin shrugged. "You didn't ask."

"But I thought you had done it and Mitzi hadn't been watching you," said Nana Potts.

"I don't make messes," Darwin said sweetly and stuck his finger in his mouth.

"You naughty little boy," said the woman. "How dare you blame my dog for something you did." She turned to Mitzi. "And you're even worse. You're old enough to know better. But you fed my dog jelly beans that could have killed her. And don't you deny it. I have the proof! You left this paper in our yard."

"That paper doesn't prove anything," interrupted Nana Potts. "Your dog took it from our porch."

The lady grabbed Mitzi by the shoulders. "I'll make you tell the truth if it's the last thing I do."

"I didn't—" Mitzi began.

"Don't lie to me!" screamed the woman. "I've seen you in our yard before. If you ever come there again, I'm going to call the police and have you arrested for trespassing."

Now it was Nana Potts' turn to scream. And her scream was louder. *"Don't you dare talk that way to my granddaughter! And if you ever walk in our house again without being asked, I'll have you arrested for trespassing!"* She raised a big mixing spoon over her head in a threatening gesture.

Impressed by his grandmother's bravery, Darwin sought a weapon, too. He grabbed her black wig, which was lying on the kitchen table like a mound of fur. Waving the wig in the woman's face, he hollered, "If you ever walk in our house again without being asked, I'll tell my raccoon to bite you!"

"EEEK!" wailed the woman and ran out the door.

Mitzi slammed the door behind her, and the three members of the Potts family burst into giggles. Then Nana Potts caught Darwin and Mitzi by the hands and began dancing and singing: "Who's afraid of the big bad witch, the big bad witch, the big bad witch—"

At last the three of them collapsed on the floor, panting. Mitzi realized that Nana Potts was smiling at her, with the same kind of smile she usually reserved for Darwin.

Mitzi smiled back shyly.

Nana Potts threw an arm around each of the children and gave them a tight squeeze. "We're a good team, aren't we?"

"We're the toughest team in town," said Darwin.

Mitzi looked at Nana Potts. She wasn't exactly the kind of grandmother Mitzi had planned on, but in a strange way, Mitzi almost liked her. "Yes," Mitzi said.

"This calls for a celebration," said Nana Potts. "Let's have a picnic."

Well. Mitzi was sure of it. She *did* like Nana Potts. A grandmother who planned picnics was a good kind of grandmother to have.

Ring! went the front doorbell. *Ring!*

"I'll get it," offered Darwin. He scampered through the dining room toward the front door. But Nana Potts and Mitzi soon overtook him.

"Milo!" exclaimed Nana Potts as she opened the front door.

"I heard all the yelling over here," said Mr. Hathaway, "and I wanted to make sure you were all right."

"Oh, we're fine," answered Nana Potts. "We were just planning a little picnic. Care to join us?"

Mr. Hathaway hesitated.

"I'll tell her to make lemon pie and peanut butter popcorn balls," said Darwin.

"All *right!*" said Mr. Hathaway, just like a teenager. "When's the big shindig, Mary Beth?"

"In a couple of hours, I guess," said Nana Potts. "It will take me a while to fry some chicken and fix the rest of the menu Darwin has in mind." She rumpled Darwin's hair.

"Perfect," said Mr. Hathaway. "That will give me time to drive Bob home and go to my apartment for a shower."

"You're not going to take the cherry picker home, are you?" Darwin asked Mr. Hathaway. "You promised to give me a ride."

"Well, we can do that another day," said Mr. Hathaway. "I thought I'd drive the cherry picker home and pick up my Bobcat."

"You'll do no such thing," said Nana Potts. "If I'm providing the food for this picnic, you'll provide the place. The children want to go up and down in the cage on your cherry picker, and so do I. That's where we'll have our picnic—up high in that cage on top of the highest hill we can find."

Mr. Hathaway grinned. "Okay. Why not?"

Oh boy, thought Mitzi. Nana Potts was not just a good kind of grandmother. She was the *best* kind.

Nana Potts'
Peanut Butter Popcorn Balls

1. Measure into a big pan with tall sides:
   3 quarts (12 cups) popped corn
2. Measure into a heavy cooking pan (such as a cast-iron pressure cooker):
   1 cup sugar
   1 cup light corn syrup
3. Bring mixture to a vigorous boil and cook 30 seconds, stirring constantly.
4. Remove cooking pan from heat and add:
   1 cup peanut butter (creamy or chunk style)
   1 teaspoon vanilla (optional)
5. Stir syrup briskly with spoon until smooth.
6. Pour syrup over popped corn in the tall pan.
7. Stir syrup through corn quickly, before syrup cools. With a long-handled spoon in each hand, mix syrup through popcorn as you would toss a salad. Work from the outsides of the mixing pan toward the center, lifting the popcorn and then dropping it gently back into the center of the pan. Count 200 strokes, until each floweret of corn is coated with syrup.

8. With a pan of lukewarm water at your side to wash your hands as needed, form popcorn into balls.

Recipe makes about 10 small popcorn balls.